moxi
the underdog

written and illustrated by
annie west

MERCIER PRESS
WHAT YOU NEED TO READ

Once upon a time there was a farm. On this farm lived a scrawny cat, three sad hens, some ill-mannered sheep and cows, and a big, cross, cranky bull.
Everyone was afraid of the bull.
One day, just as the sun was coming up, the animals heard a noise outside in the lane.

Bump bump ... Thump ... Slam! ... Vroooommmm

Cat and hens crept out to see what it was.

There in the middle of the lane was a dusty grey sack tied at the top with blue string.

Cat and hens sniffed the bag. It smelt bad, like burnt cabbage.

Cat gave the sack a nudge with his paw. The bag began to move.

Cat and hens jumped back with fright.
Just then Farmer Bob appeared. He took out his
penknife and cut the string.

Out jumped a scruffy, dusty little dog.
'Hello,' said Cat.
'How do you do?' said the dog,
with a smile and a bow. 'The
name's Moxie. What a lovely farm
you have. I am so pleased to be
here. Actually, I'm pleased to be
anywhere.'
'What a funny little fellow,' said the
hens.
'And very polite,' whispered the cat.
Farmer Bob fed and washed Moxie
and went away to feed the cows.

Moxie began to explore the farmyard. Cat and hens followed. They listened as he told them his story.

'I may be small and scruffy, but don't be fooled by my looks. I was born humble and didn't have a chance in life. But my mum always said to me, "Moxie, you are small and scrawny. You are an underdog. You will have a hard life. Be brave. If everything goes wrong and you feel like giving up, just keep trying. Always remember I love you".'

Cat and hens smiled.

'Tell us more, Moxie,' they said.

'I've been here, there and everywhere. I've been bitten, beaten, mocked and ridiculed. I've been misled, sold out and shot at. I've been cheated, defeated, kicked around and scorned. And now, today, I've been thrown out, dumped and left for dead. I really am an underdog.'

'Have you ever given up?' asked the hens.

'Not yet!' said Moxie with a smile.

Moxie met the cows, and the sheep. They laughed at him because he was small and had a bite out of one ear and a bullet hole in the other ear. Bits of his fur were missing and he walked with a limp. Moxie was sad, but he didn't show it. Instead he smiled and said, 'I may be small and bits of me are missing; but I have a big heart and good manners. I won't find fault with you even though you are laughing at me.'

The cows and sheep had nothing to say.

Later that day Moxie found himself outside a big shed. He could hear a loud roaring and banging sound. A huge brown creature stood looking at him. Steam was coming out of the creature's nose. It was Bull. Moxie was frightened, but he didn't show it.

'What do YOU want?' said Bull. 'Look at you. You're small and useless. What could Farmer Bob want YOU for?' Bull stamped hard on Moxie's tail.

Moxie's tail was flattened.

'Your words hurt me as much as your hooves,' said Moxie. 'But I have been hurt before. I'll pay no attention.'

Cat and hens looked on, afraid.
Cat said, 'Oh he's terrible and
cranky. And mean. He always
makes fun of me. He says I can't
catch mice because I'm small and
useless.'

'You're not small and useless,'
said Moxie. 'You have fine silky fur
and sharp clean teeth. You have
guts. You are honest and truthful.'

Moxie winked and said, 'Can a
bull catch a rat?'

'You know, you're right,' said
Cat, feeling better already. 'I do my
best. I may be small and scrawny
but I'm good at being a cat. I won't
give up yet.'

Later the same day Moxie was walking in the yard. Bull was on his way
to the field with Farmer Bob.

Baff!

Moxie was thrown up in the air by a kick from Bull's huge hooves.
Cat and hens were afraid.

'Are you going to give up?' said the hens, as Moxie landed, **splat,**
in a big puddle.

'Not yet!' said Moxie, dripping with muck and dirty water.

As Bull walked down the yard he shoved the hens out of the way with his enormous nose.

'We wish he would stop doing that. He's a bully. He says we're dirty birds and can't lay enough eggs. He thinks we're small and useless.'

'You're not small and useless,' said Moxie. 'Look at your beautiful golden feathers. You have grit and good manners.' Moxie winked and said, 'Can a bull lay an egg?'

'You're right Moxie,' said the hens, feeling better already. 'We do our best. We are good at being hens. We won't give up yet.'

Every day when Bull went out he chased after Moxie and kicked him or pushed him or stood on him. He called him names and made fun of him.

Biff! 'Stupid dog.'

Blatch! 'You're useless.'

Splat! 'I'm bigger than you.'

'Please give up!' yelled the hens, as Moxie flew through the air once more.
'Not yet!' said Moxie.

One day Farmer Bob opened the gate to bring Bull
for his walk. Just then Bull pushed past Farmer Bob
and ran down the yard, kicking and roaring and
being scary. Everybody ran.
Everybody but Moxie.
Farmer Bob was trapped against the wall and could
not escape. He was scared but didn't show it. Moxie
ran up to Bull and grabbed his tail between his
teeth. Bull was mad.

Moxie was thrown up and down as Bull tried to shake him off, but Moxie only held on tighter.

'Will-you-let-GO!!!' roared Bull.

'Not yet!' yelled Moxie, through his teeth.

Farmer Bob quickly moved and got Bull into the shed, banging the door shut. But still Moxie would not let go.

Sheep and cows called from the field. They thought Moxie was brave and fearless (and very polite).

'Moxie!' they yelled, 'have you given up yet?'

'Not yet!' said Moxie.

It was late that night, and Bull was in his shed. Moxie still held on to his tail.

'When will you let go of my tail?' said Bull, feeling very tired and sore.

'When you say you are sorry,' said Moxie.

Bull could not sleep. He thought about how Moxie had held on even though he was scared and tired and sore. Moxie might be small and scruffy but he was brave. Bull felt bad for being mean to him.

He turned to Moxie and said, 'I'm sorry. I promise I won't forget my manners. I'll stop being mean to the other animals. I won't attack Farmer Bob again.'

'That's very decent of you, Bull,' said Moxie, letting go of Bull's tail at last. 'You are good at being a bull. You are strong and powerful. You don't have to be mean because you are big.'

At dawn the next morning Moxie crept out of the shed. He was still tired and very sore, and more bits of him were missing. He lifted his head and sniffed the air.

'I smell another adventure,' said Moxie.

He woke the animals and told them it was time for him to go.

All the animals were sad.

'Don't worry,' said Moxie. 'I'll be back soon. Say goodbye to Farmer Bob for me.'

'We will,' said all the animals.

The animals watched as Moxie trotted out into the lane.

The last thing they saw was Moxie jumping on the back of a big circus truck as it went by.

The animals all missed Moxie, and his bravery.

Bull was still big and scary, but he never attacked anyone again.

Cat was better at catching mice.

Hens laid more eggs than ever.

When the animals had babies – chicks, calves and lambs – they would tell them their favourite story at bedtime, all about the adventures of Moxie the Underdog. How he tried and tried and never gave up.

And in the shed beside them, listening carefully, was Bull, who loved that story most of all.

Moxie
the
underdog

Inspired by Irish rugby hero Peter Stringer

MERCIER PRESS

Trade enquiries ... ... ackrock, County Dublin

This book is sold subject to the condition t... ... t the publisher's prior consent in any form of binding
or cover other than that in which it is publis... ...aser. No part of this publication may be reproduced or
transmitted in any form or by any means, el... ...ithout the prior permission of the publisher in writing.